THE BRASS RING

NANCY TAFURI

GREENWILLOW BOOKS • NEW YORK

For Cristina

The carousel pictured in this book is The Flying Horse Carousel in Watch Hill, Rhode Island, one of the oldest carousels in the United States.

Colored pencils, watercolors, and a black pen were used for the full-color art. The text type is Adobe Garamond.

Printed in Singapore by Tien Wah Press
First Edition 10 9 8 7 6 5 4 3 2 1

Library of Congress
Cataloging-in-Publication Data

Tafuri, Nancy.
The brass ring / by Nancy Tafuri.
   p.   cm.
Summary: Being on vacation is even more fun for one who is bigger and can do more things such as ride a bike, float and swim, and buy a carousel ticket.
ISBN 0-688-14168-4 (trade).
ISBN 0-688-14169-2 (lib. bdg.)
[1. Vacations—Fiction.
2. Growth—Fiction.
3. Size—Fiction.]   I. Title.
PZ7.T117Br   1996   [E]—dc20
95-25084   CIP   AC

I like being big. When I was little, I really didn't know what vacations were. I would sleep in the car instead of asking, "Are we there yet?"

When I was little,
I couldn't say hello
to everyone when
we arrived or
run to the beach.

Now I can ride my bicycle and meet new friends.

When I was little,
I couldn't float on
my back or swim.

I couldn't
race a wave
or build a
sand castle.

Now that I am big,
I can find
sea stars and
snails.

I can dig
for clams and
scoop up
rock crabs.

But now what I like best
about vacations is the carousel.

Now I am big enough
to buy my own ticket.

I stand in line until my
favorite outside horse is free.

He is white and silver
with a red saddle.
I call him Thunder.

The music starts.
I hold the pole and
ride like the wind!

I watch for the
brass ring and
lean out far.
Can I get it?

YES !
I've won

another ride !

I like being BIG !